W9-DCL-397

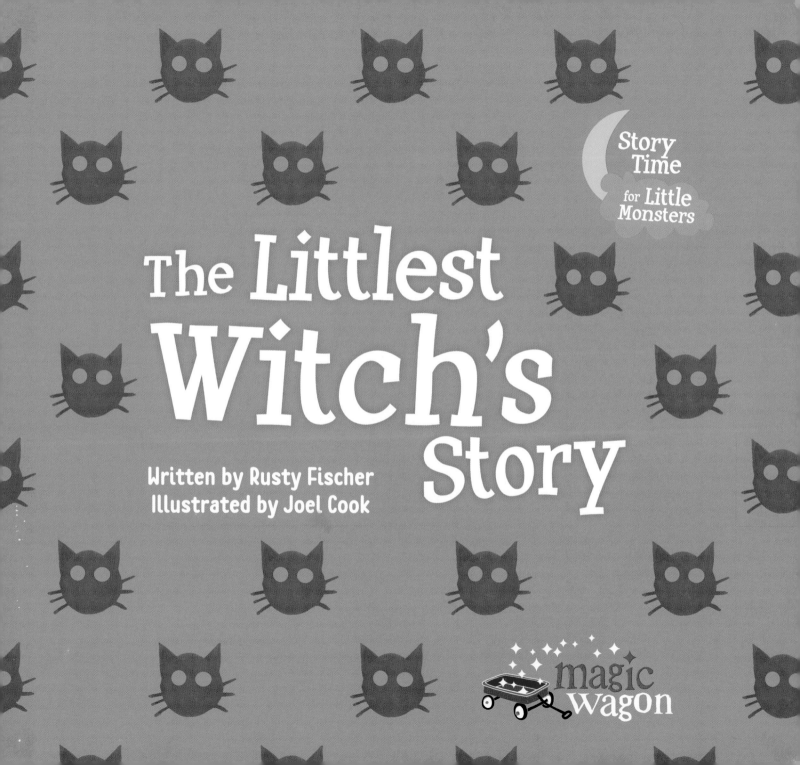

Story Time for Little Monsters

The Littlest Witch's Story

Written by Rusty Fischer
Illustrated by Joel Cook

magic wagon

visit us at www.abdopublishing.com

Published by Magic Wagon, a division of the ABDO Group, PO Box 398166, Minneapolis, MN 55439.
Copyright © 2014 by Abdo Consulting Group, Inc. International copyrights reserved in all countries.
All rights reserved. No part of this book may be reproduced in any form without written permission
from the publisher.

Looking Glass Library™ is a trademark and logo of Magic Wagon.

Printed in the United States of America, North Mankato, Minnesota.
102013
012014

 This book contains at least 10% recycled materials.

Written by Rusty Fischer
Illustrations by Joel Cook
Edited by Stephanie Hedlund and Rochelle Baltzer
Cover and interior design by Renée LaViolette and Candice Keimig

Library of Congress Cataloging-in-Publication Data

Fischer, Rusty, author.
  The littlest witch's story / written by Rusty Fischer ; illustrated by Joel Cook.
     pages cm. -- (Story time for little monsters)
  Summary: Told in rhyming text, little Winnie the Witch wants to fly her broom, but the sleeping spell
she tries to cast on her mother backfires.
  ISBN 978-1-62402-022-3
1. Witches--Juvenile fiction. 2. Mothers and daughters--Juvenile fiction. 3. Bedtime--Juvenile fiction.
4. Stories in rhyme. [1. Stories in rhyme. 2. Witches--Fiction. 3. Mothers and daughters--Fiction. 4.
Bedtime--Fiction.] I. Cook, Joel, illustrator. II. Title.
  PZ8.3.F62854Lk 2014
  813.6--dc23   2013025329

Winnie the Witch would not go to sleep.
She would not even try.
She stared at her broom in the corner
and couldn't wait
until she could fly.

She'd zoom overhead and fly through the night as the town grew tiny below.
But she'd have to sneak out, for if she were to ask, her mother was sure to say, "No."

So Winnie the Witch had cast a spell upon her witchy mother,
whose only goal in life, it seemed, was to gloat and haunt and smother.

She never let her fly for fun
or cast cool, witchy spells.
She couldn't snoop around in jars
and vials with awful, witchy smel

As darkness fell upon the land,
Little Winnie smiled and waited.
Her mother paced and walked the
floor, growing weary and frustrated.

"I wish you'd come and settle down," Winnie's mother did say. "For sleep is what awaits us, dear, at the end of a busy day."

"But I'm not tired," our Winnie whined, as her mother paced the floor. Winnie smirked and waited for her mother's first loud snore.

"Let's both lie down," our Winnie said as she hung her witch hat up. But Mother just stood right there and studied her empty cup.

"My tea tasted funny," Mother frowned
as she stirred the bubbling cauldron.
"Are you sure you used the tea bags from
the tin above the oven?"

"Of course I did." Winnie did yawn as she climbed right into bed. She wasn't tired, but it wouldn't hurt to rest her head.

Soon Winnie could not keep her eyes open as the room did swirl. And Mother dear, she danced and smiled and gave a little twirl.

"I'm sleepy, Mother." Winnie yawned.
"And I don't see quite why.
You should be yawning, Mother dear,
as the moonlight fills the sky."

Winnie frowned at her mother's words. "You knew?" she asked out loud. "I thought I'd tricked you, Mom, at last. Of myself I was quite proud."

"As you should be," her mom did say as she tucked her daughter in. "If I hadn't tasted eye of newt, I'd be sure to pack it in."

"I drank your potion, little one,"
Winnie's mom said with a smile.
"But then I cast a reversal spell
from mother to her child."

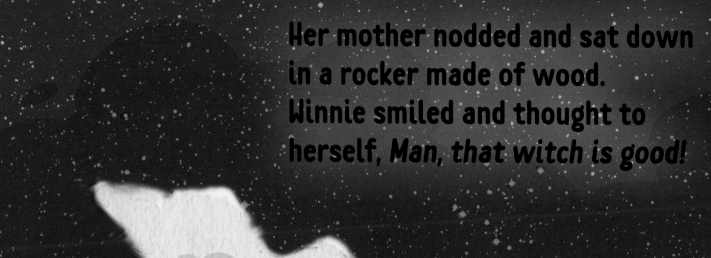

Her mother nodded and sat down
in a rocker made of wood.
Winnie smiled and thought to
herself, *Man, that witch is good!*